I Can Trick a Tiger

Cynthia Rider • Alex Brychta

OXFORD

UNIVERSITY PRESS

Floppy was dreaming that
he was in the jungle.

A tiger jumped out.
"Got you!" he said.

"I can trick a tiger,"
said Floppy.

"Look out!" said Floppy.
"There's a bee on your nose."

"Oh no!" said the tiger,
and he let Floppy go.

A crocodile jumped out.
"Got you!" she said.

"I can trick a crocodile,"
said Floppy.

"Look out!" said Floppy.
"There's a bee on your nose."

"Oh no!" said the crocodile,
and she let Floppy go.

A snake slid out.

"Got you!" she said.

"I can trick a snake,"
said Floppy.

"Look out!" said Floppy.
"There's a bee on your nose."

"Oh no!" said the snake,
and she let Floppy go.

A rabbit jumped out.
"Got you!" said Floppy.

"Look out!" said the rabbit.
"There's a bee on your nose."

Buzzzzzzzz!
"Oh no!" said Floppy.

Why did
the tiger let
Floppy go?

What would you
do if you had a
bee on your nose?

How do you think
Floppy felt when the bee
landed on his nose?

Have you
ever played a trick
on anybody?

Was it a funny
trick?

Rhyming words

Match the things that rhyme.

More books for you to enjoy

Level 1: Getting Ready

Level 2: Starting to Read

Level 3: Becoming a Reader

Level 4: Building Confidence

OXFORD
UNIVERSITY PRESS

Great Clarendon Street,
Oxford OX2 6DP

Text © Cynthia Rider 2005
Illustrations © Alex Brychta 2005
Designed by Andy Wilson

First published 2005

ISBN 0 19 838558 7

10 9 8 7 6 5 4 3 2 1

Printed in China by Imago

Tips for Reading Together

Children learn best when reading is fun.

- Talk about the title and the pictures on the cover.
- Look through the pictures together and discuss what you think the story might be about.
- Read the story together, pointing to the words and inviting your child to join in.
- Give lots of praise as your child reads with you, and help them when necessary.
- Have fun finding the hidden tree frog.
- Enjoy re-reading the story and encourage your child to say the repeated phrases with you.

Children enjoy reading stories again and again.
This helps to build their confidence.

Have fun!

Find the tree frog hidden in every picture.